Hey Jack! Books

First American Edition 2015
Kane Miller, A Division of EDC Publishing

Text copyright © 2014 Sally Rippin
Illustration copyright © 2014 Stephanie Spartels
First published in Australia in 2014 by Hardie Grant Egmont

For information contact:
Kane Miller, A Division of EDC Publishing
P.O. Box 470663
Tulsa, OK 74147-0663
www.kanemiller.com
www.edcpub.com
www.usbornebooksandmore.com

Library of Congress Control Number: 2014950307

Printed and bound in the United States of America
3 4 5 6 7 8 9 10

ISBN: 978-1-61067-394-5

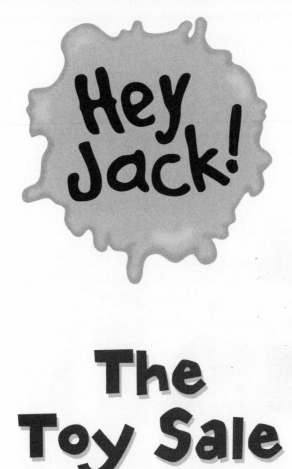

The
Toy Sale

By Sally Rippin

Illustrated by Stephanie Spartels

Kane Miller
A DIVISION OF EDC PUBLISHING

Chapter One

This is Jack. Today Jack is in a busy mood. He is making a shop! Jack is going to sell some of his old toys in his shop.

He wants to make enough money for a trading card folder.

Jack sorts through his toy box. He finds lots of toys he has forgotten about. He starts to sort them into piles.

Soon, Jack has three piles of toys. One pile to sell. One pile to keep.

And one little pile of toys he is not sure about.

Jack looks at this pile for a long time. There are some good toys in there.

Slowly he sorts through the pile, putting some in the pile to sell and some in the pile to keep.

Soon, there is only one toy left. It is a robot dog. Jack only got the dog last Christmas. It used to **bark** and do **flips**. But it has stopped working.

4

Jack holds the robot dog.
He is not sure what to
do with it.

At last, he puts the dog
on the pile to sell. It is
really not very fun now
that it doesn't work.

Jack sets up a table in
front of his garage.
He puts all the toys he is
selling out on the table.

Jack writes a sign like this:

Toys For Sale!

Then he begins writing price tags to put on the toys.

Just then, Billie wanders over from next door. She looks at the toys on the table.

6

"Do you want to buy anything?" asks Jack.

Billie shrugs. "Maybe." Then she spots Jack's robot dog.

"Wow. Are you selling that?" she says. She sounds surprised.

"It doesn't work anymore," Jack says.

Billie lifts up the dog. "Maybe it needs new batteries?"

"I tried that," Jack says.

"How much?" Billie says.

Jack thinks. He hasn't
decided yet.

"Well, it is probably the
best toy here," he says.
"So it costs … ten dollars."

Billie looks disappointed. "I don't have that much money," she says **sadly**. "But Rebecca might! She's coming over this afternoon."

"Cool!" says Jack. "Bring her to see my shop."

Jack finishes writing all the price tags.

Then he sits behind
the table to wait for
customers. But nobody
comes.

Jack's dog, Scraps, comes over with a ball in his mouth.

"Not now, Scraps," says Jack. "I'm busy."

Jack begins to feel bored. He yawns. *Hurry up, Billie!* he thinks. *I need some customers!*

Chapter Two

Finally, Jack sees a car pull up outside Billie's house. Rebecca steps out of the car. Billie rushes out to meet her.

"Hi, Rebecca!" Jack calls.

"Hey, Jack!" Rebecca
waves. "What are you
doing?"

"Running a toy shop,"
says Jack. "Come and
look!"

Billie and Rebecca
run over.

"Wow. That's a cool
robot dog," Rebecca
says. "How much is it?"

"Ten dollars," Jack says.

Rebecca frowns. "That's
a lot of money, Jack,"
she says.

Jack shrugs. "It's a good toy. Maybe there's something else here you'd like to buy?" he says.

Rebecca picks up some of the other toys.

Jack knows that nothing is as good as the robot dog.

"Come on, Jack," Billie says. "Rebecca is a friend. You should give her a good price."

"I can give you two of these Lego men for half price," Jack suggests.

But Rebecca shakes her head. "I have lots of Lego already." She pulls out her wallet and counts out her money.

"I only have seven dollars and fifty cents,"

she says. "Will you give me the robot dog for that much?"

"Um…" says Jack.

Billie glares at Jack.
"It doesn't even work,
Jack," she reminds him.

"Well, all right," Jack says
slowly. "I guess so."

He takes the money
and hands Rebecca the
robot dog.

"Yay, it's so cute!"
Rebecca says.

"Come on, Billie. Let's go and play with it at your house."

The two girls run off with the robot dog.

Jack watches them go.
He looks down at the
money. He knows he
should feel happy. It is
his first and only sale.

Now he only needs
three more dollars to
have enough for his
trading card folder.

But for some reason

Jack feels **strange**.

He is not really sure he

wanted to sell that robot

dog.

Chapter Three

Jack sits at his shop all afternoon. Scraps lies under the table with the ball next to him. Scraps looks **sad**.

Jack would like to go and play with him, but he needs to stay and look after his shop.

Two kids from across the road come and visit the shop.

One buys a Lego man for fifty cents. The other pays one dollar for Jack's old Star Wars cup.

They look happy with their new things.

Jack waits and waits.
But no more customers
come. He begins to get
bored again.

So he writes another
sign like this:

Back in 15 minutes!

Jack can hear Billie
and Rebecca playing
in Billie's backyard.
He wanders out into his
backyard to see if he can
find out what they are
up to.

They are laughing and **squealing**. But there is another sound, too. A metallic barking sound. It sounds just like a robot dog!

Jack peeks through the hole in the fence. Billie spots him.

"Look, Jack!" she shouts.

"We got it working! You just put the batteries in the wrong way."

"Isn't it cute?" Rebecca laughs. "Look! It jumps up and down. Just like a real puppy."

Billie and Rebecca are having lots of **fun** with the robot dog.

Suddenly Jack wishes
he hadn't sold the robot
dog after all.

"I didn't know it still
worked!" he says crossly.
"I wouldn't have sold it
if I knew that!"

Billie shrugs. "It's
Rebecca's now," she says.

"That's not fair!" Jack shouts. "It's worth much more than seven dollars and fifty cents!"

The girls glare back.

"It is too fair!" says Rebecca.

Jack feels his head fizzing with anger. *I should never have started that stupid shop!* he thinks. Then he runs up to his bedroom and crawls under his bed.

36

This is a quiet place
he likes to hide when
things feel too hard.

Jack tries to think of a way
to get the robot dog back.

*I could take the robot
dog back when they are
not looking,* he thinks.
No, that would be stealing.

*Maybe I could swap it for
another toy?* he wonders.
*No, there's no other toys
I want to give away.*

*I could give Rebecca back
her money,* he thinks.
*But then I won't have
enough money to buy
the folder.*

Just then, Jack feels
a warm furry body
squeeze in next to him.
He feels a soft wet
tongue on his cheek.

39

He giggles and gives his dog, Scraps, a big cuddle. He feels his anger melt away.

Jack realizes that he doesn't really want the robot dog back.

He never really played with it much anyway.

Jack has a real dog. And that's a hundred times better than a robot one!

41

"Come on, Scraps," says Jack. "Let's go and play ball!"

Collect them all!

Friendship is one of our most valuable gifts. It completes our desire to realize our capacity to love. It brings to our lives that closeness that makes us feel connected and whole and that lets us know we are not alone in the world.

Titles by Marci
Published by
Blue Mountain Arts®

Friends Are Forever
A Gift of Inspirational Thoughts
to Thank You for Being
My Friend

10 Simple Things
to Remember
An Inspiring Guide to
Understanding Life

To My Daughter
Love and Encouragement
to Carry with You on Your
Journey Through Life

To My Mother
I Will Always Carry
Your Love in My Heart

To My Sister
A Gift of Love and Inspiration
to Thank You
for Being My Sister

You Are My "Once in a Lifetime"
I Will Always Love You

Friends Are Forever

A Gift of Inspirational Thoughts
to Thank You for Being
My Friend

Marci

Blue Mountain Press™
Boulder, Colorado

Dedicated to my sister Jeri
who is always there with whatever
I need and is my best friend.
I love you!

Copyright © 2011 by Marci.

All rights reserved. No part of this publication may be reproduced, stored in a retrieval system or transmitted in any form or by any means, electronic, mechanical, photocopying, recording or otherwise, without the written permission of the publisher.

Library of Congress Control Number: 2010917474
ISBN: 978-1-59842-601-4

Children of the Inner Light is a registered trademark. Used under license.
Certain trademarks are used under license.

Printed in China.
Ninth Printing: 2014

⊕ This book is printed on recycled paper.

This book is printed on paper that has been specially produced to be acid free (neutral pH) and contains no groundwood or unbleached pulp. It conforms with the requirements of the American National Standards Institute, Inc., so as to ensure that this book will last and be enjoyed by future generations.

Blue Mountain Arts, Inc.

P.O. Box 4549, Boulder, Colorado 80306

contents

Friends Are Forever

We Have Shared
So Much Through
the Years

Each time I see you, I am reminded of how special our friendship is. It doesn't seem to matter how long it has been between visits, as we pick up right where we left off. We have shared so much through the years... our hopes, our dreams, our joys, and our struggles. Thank you for being a part of my life.

I'll Always
Be Grateful

for Our Friendship

As I travel my journey through life, I try to remember to be grateful for the things that are really important. I want you to know that one of the greatest blessings in my life is my friendship with you. You are the person I call when I need to talk, and I know that you will be there sometimes to "just listen." You are the person that I can laugh with about the most important life events. You "know me," and that saves words sometimes... I'm so grateful to share a friendship with you.

You Will Always
Have a Place

in My Heart

Our hearts have grown closer with the passing of time. Through the ups and downs of life, we've come to understand what it means to have each other. Sometimes we talk often... sometimes not. It doesn't seem to matter — the feelings of closeness remain with me because I know you are always there. What a blessing it is to have you in my life.

Some people have a way of brightening someone's day... and it's with little things that mean so much. There is a phone call at just the right time, a hug when it is needed, or a comforting word of encouragement.

That special person is you!
Your Kind and generous
spirit shines brightly in my
life. Thank you for all you
do and all you are.

I could Never Find a Better Friend

...Than You

If I searched the world,
I could never find a better
friend. You are a perfect
example of loving and caring
and compassion and concern.
Just talking to you makes
me feel better, and being
with you reminds me of the
most important things in life.
Knowing that I have a friend
like you is truly wonderful!

You're Always There When I Need You

Some days I just need a hand to hold... Some days I just need a hug... Some days I just need a word of encouragement... Some days I just need someone to be there for a laugh and a memory... On my "some days" there is you!

Wherever I go... whatever I do... I carry your friendship in my heart. You give me hope and make life's challenges bearable. You inspire me to do my best. Your friendship stays in my heart each and every hour of the day and reminds me that I am not alone.

An Angel Has Blessed
My Life

...With Your Friendship

The blessings of an angel come in many ways. Sometimes these gifts are right before us, and it is only through time that we realize just how blessed we are. You are always there to share a laugh, and you are always ready to tell me everything will be okay when I'm down. I have come to appreciate these simple blessings. You are an angel in my life.

You and I, my friend, are two hearts traveling in the same direction. We have one of those rare connections that gives us such a beautiful relationship. So often you know my thoughts before I say them or sense what I need before I ask. Surely God's infinite plan has put you in my path... and selected you to be my friend!

You Are Everything a Friend Should Be ...and More

A friend's love is a gift that you unwrap a little bit each year.

A friend is a mirror of things to come and a reflection of things gone by.

A friend shows you the road before you and knows the path you've taken.

A friend is the one you call when you need to talk to someone who knows your heart.

A friend walks beside you to share each day... stands beside you when you question yourself... and walks in front of you when you've lost your way.

A friend sees your beautiful spirit shining through on good days and bad.

I'm so glad you are my friend!

There Is a Reason

Our Lives Were
Brought Together

You are always ready to share with me your experience, strength, and hope, and when I need your guidance, you offer me your wisdom and your understanding. You are there through the good times and a constant light through the bad. When I think about the things that are important to me, I always think of you.

I Treasure
Your Presence

in My Life

I have watched you cultivate your unique talents and have been inspired to do the same. I have watched you live with integrity, and this example has led the way. I have accepted the challenge to be my best self, as your encouraging words lifted me up. Watching you handle the ups and downs of life, and seeing you move always to higher ground, gives me a vision of my future.

Friendship Means...

Friendship means never having to face the challenges of life alone.

Friendship means sharing a closeness of spirit that gives life meaning.

Friendship means having a witness to life's tiny, special moments that are so much better when shared.

Friendship means that there is someone who understands where you've been, knows where you want to go, and accepts you for who you are.

Thank you for all that you give so freely and for showing me the true meaning of friendship!

Our Friendship

Was Meant to Be

A lifetime yields only a few lasting friendships. It happens when two special people meet and connect heart and soul. There develops an understanding of what is in each other's heart that transcends words... there is a nurturing of the spirit that is mutual... there is an exchange of love and support that is essential... and there is a sense of belonging and knowing that their friendship was meant to be.

It's Rare to Find
a Friend

as Special as You

So many times I think of you,
and I experience all over again
the special times we have had.
I remember a laugh we shared,
and I smile; I remember the love
and support you offered, and I
feel thankful. I think about
how important friendships are
in a world where everything else
seems so uncertain, and I know
I am truly blessed! Good friends
like you are a rare treasure. It
is a gift to have you as mine!

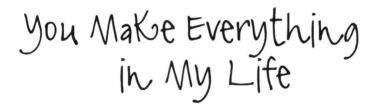

You Make Everything
in My Life

So Much Better

You are there with love,
encouragement, or a hug,
and somehow you always seem
to know just what I need.
When I am down, you lift me
up, forgiving my mistakes and
helping me forget them, too...
When I need encouragement,
you let me know that I
am not alone...

When I need a hug, you wrap
your arms around me and tell me
everything will be okay... When
there are good times, we laugh
and they are so much better...
and when we share sorrow, it
seems half as bad.

When I look back, I realize
that you had such an impact
on my life — one you may not
have realized. I want you to
know that your kind spirit and
loving heart have touched me
in a special way with a lasting
impression called friendship!

You're More Than a Friend...

This
❤
Way
❤
Home
❤

You're like Family

You have taught me that what makes a "family" is not found in a name, it is found in the heart. You are so much more to me than a friend... you are like family. You are always there, believing in my dreams and reminding me to believe in them. You are a part of every joy that comes my way, and I am so happy to have you in my life.

You Are That One
Special Friend to Me

I Don't Know What
I'd Do Without You

We all need that one special person to connect with in a way that transcends ordinary friendship. We need that special someone with whom we can share life's innermost secrets. We need that friend to laugh with over absolutely nothing, and we need to know a hug is ready and waiting on the worst of days. I can find all of these things in you... you are that one special friend to me.

I'm So Glad We Have Each Other

When I think of you, I think, "What could be better than having someone to talk to who already knows all about me and loves me as I am?"

When I think of you, I think, "What could be more fun than sharing my joys with someone who is truly happy for me?"

When I think of you, I think,
"What could be better than a
friendship that has created so
many wonderful memories?"

When I think of you, I think,
"We're friends!" and I realize
how lucky I am to have you!

We Share a
Special Connection

Our Bond Is Everlasting

Some days you come into my mind just as the phone rings... and it is you! It is as though you heard or felt my thoughts and knew I needed to talk. Your timely phone call reminds me you are always there, and your understanding reminds me of what a good friend you are. Thank you for loving me... thank you for making me laugh... and thank you for the special connection we share. The bond we have found is everlasting!

My Hopes for you...

May the good things you have brought to my life be returned to you.

May your guardian angel always watch over you and whisper life's secrets in your ear.

May your steps be guided through all of life's challenges and your heart remember its true calling.

May you be blessed with all the things that will bring you lasting happiness.

May faith guide your path
toward your dreams... may hope
be a constant light in your
life... and may love warm your
heart every day.

The Road of Life Has Many Turns

Just Take It One Day at a Time

Sometimes the road of life takes us to a place we had planned... Sometimes it shows us a surprise around the bend we could never have anticipated. We make decisions based on the information we have... We accept the ups and downs as they come... We live "one day at a time"... But often we find it is only when we look back that we can see that what we had thought was a "wrong turn" has brought us to exactly the right place and every step was a right one after all!

Remember These Things...

Remember, you are special... there are talents locked away inside you just waiting for the right time to unfold.

Remember to dream... dreams are the start of every great adventure. When you close your eyes and imagine your "happy and successful self in the future," you are beginning your journey!

Remember to listen to your heart... your heart is where your courage lies. When you follow your heart you may meet challenges, but each of your steps will be guided.

Remember, "today" is always the most important day... enjoy every moment of it.

You Are an Inspiration
to So Many

...but Especially to Me

Everyone needs someone to look up to... a model of how to find one's calling and follow that dream! You are such an inspiration to so many... You have demonstrated how to move forward in spite of obstacles... how to stay the course when things get tough... and how to keep close to your heart the things that are really important in life on the journey toward success. You have shown that with determination, commitment, and a willingness to share, all your dreams will come true!

Always Follow
Your Dream

Your life holds for you endless possibilities. You have built a solid foundation, and you have worked hard for it. Continue to do what is necessary to move forward one day at a time. Write down your dream and tuck it away — entrusting that all things will come at the right time.

Keep sight always of what is important in life. Remember that true happiness and purpose will be found in relationships — in the workplace and at home. Live each day open to guidance, and your purpose will be revealed to you. May your future be filled with love and acceptance.

I Am Proud
to call You

My Friend

You handle life's ups and downs with grace and even remember to encourage others along the way. You face challenges with courage, compassion, and conviction. I am proud to call you my friend.

Kindred Spirits

That's What We Are!

Some things change with time...
some things never do. The way
I feel when I spend time with
you is one of those constant good
things in my life. There is a sense of
feeling understood... there is a sense
of feeling loved and supported... and
there is a deep sense of gratitude
as I realize I have been given the
wonderful gift of a kindred spirit.
Thank you for staying close to my
heart... thank you for a friendship
that endures... and thank you for
sharing your beautiful spirit with me.

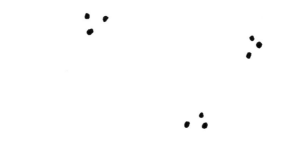

You always understand what
is in my heart. You are there
whenever I need you, listening
and offering your insights. You
look deeply enough to really see
me, allowing me to understand
the true meaning of friendship.

It's friends like you who remind me that life's most precious gifts are free. The memories that we create fulfill the promise of love. Thank you for each and every day that you have been my friend and for the memories that live in my heart forever.

You Are Always
in My Prayers

May God's Love Be
With You Always

You are always in my prayers, and I wanted you to know so that you will be open to the grace that comes your way. I have asked that you feel the love of God like a gentle breeze when you need inspiration... that your faith remain unwavering through all of life's challenges... and that hope be the burning light that always guides your way.

If you ever get discouraged, remember I am thinking of you... believing in you... praying for you... and hoping you know that no matter how big a problem seems or how hopeless you feel, you are never alone, as God's grace is only one request away!

We may not always know the right thing to do or the right path to take, but "faith" will show us the way. Remember that we are never alone, as God is always there to answer prayers and send us the help we need. Sometimes it is "we" who do not recognize that help. Believe, trust, and pray... and know that all your needs will be taken care of.

Dear Friend

You Are Stronger
Than You Realize

There are times in our lives when we face a hardship that we do not think we can bear. We wonder, "Why," and we look for a reason to help make sense of it all. Sometimes all we can do is try to come to a place of acceptance and reach out to others who understand what we've been through. Often it is then, as we share our wisdom, strength, and hope, that we get a small glimpse of a larger plan... one that enables us to feel connected... one that shows us that love blesses the giver and the receiver... and one that allows us to see how really strong we are.

Five Keys
to Happiness

1. Realize that happiness is a choice... you can make the decision to "be happy" each day.

2. Remember that happiness is contagious. Make someone smile, and the good feelings come right back to you.

3. Be grateful for the little things in life that are free. Make a list, and add to it each morning.

4. Believe that ultimately everything happens for a reason. Acceptance leads the way to happiness.

5. Give away some courage every day! When you encourage another to "keep going," "hang in there," or "believe in their dreams," you will find an unending source of happiness.

Big problems can be solved in small steps.

When you are still, the gentle voice from within will guide you... listen carefully.

Remember to pray, and let God take the burden of worry from your heart.

Accept that we each learn life's lessons in our own way.

Your Friendship Is like
an Angel's Wings...

Lifting Me Up at
Just the Right Time

You are always there... to help me fix the bad things, appreciate the little things, and remind me that the most important things in life are free! Your encouraging words and your faith in me are gifts beyond measure.

In today's world, life gets so busy that the days roll by and we realize we have not spoken to the ones we love! I want you to know that you are always in my heart... You are one of the most important people in my life, and even if we do not speak every day, my best thoughts and love are always with you.

It is easy to lose track of time. The days pass, and then one day we realize we have lost touch with someone special. So often you are in my thoughts, and I smile thinking of the many memories we have shared. I treasure our talks and our special connection.

Just know that neither time nor distance changes the closeness I feel in my heart when I think of you. You are such an important part of my life... always ready to be part of whatever is happening... always open to listening... always there to share a laugh or dry some tears. And I am always so grateful to have you as my friend!

No Matter What...

I Want Us to
Always Stay close

Friendship is one of life's greatest treasures, and it is a gift that lasts a lifetime. We created a bond during a time in our lives when our beliefs and our experiences were shaping who we were. That bond cannot be broken by the passing of time, even when life gets so busy that we lose touch. I want you to know I think of you often... and you will always have a special place in my heart.

Longtime Friends

Time Spent with Friends
creates Lifelong
Sweet Memories

Every time we're together, precious moments come flooding back, and I am reminded of all our laughter and joy through the years. I am so appreciative of those times and for having met you. Through the pain and sorrow, happiness and joy, we have learned much. Yours is the humor I can always count on and the friendship I know will last forever.

My Wishes for you

I wish you a life filled with love... a true love to share your every dream... family love to warm your heart... and priceless love found in the gift of friendship.

I wish you peace... peace in knowing who you are... peace in knowing what you believe in... and peace in the understanding of what is important in life.

I wish you joy... joy as you awaken each day with gratitude in your heart for new beginnings... joy when you surrender to the beauty of a flower or a baby's smile... and joy, a hundred times returned, for each time you've brought happiness to another's heart.

Thanks

for All the Little Things You Do

Sometimes I forget to say "thanks" for all the little things you do... but I want you to know that even when I do not say so, I am so thankful for your thoughtfulness, your caring, your willingness to please. Your efforts never go unnoticed, and I thank you!

Your Friendship
Has Made

Such a Difference
in My Life

There are people who change our lives, often without even realizing the impact they have made just by being themselves. You have made such a difference in my life. I am grateful for the way you are always willing to share the precious gift of time... for always believing in the best in people... for always seeing the bright side of things... for the many kind words you have spoken... for the thoughtful things you have done... The world needs more people like you!

Imagine me wrapping my arms around you with my heart. I am so happy that you are a part of my life! Consider yourself hugged!

You Are a Friend

Friend

I Will Always Cherish

When I think of our friendship, I realize that it is one of the things I cherish the most in my life. It is hard to put into words a "thank you" with enough meaning for all the times you have come through for me... for all the times you have listened instead of telling me what to do... for all the times you have hugged away my troubles... for the laughs over nothing... for the many tears dried. Thank you for it all, my special, cherished friend!

About Marci

Marci began her career by hand painting floral designs on clothing. No one was more surprised than she was when one day, in a single burst of inspiration and a completely new and different art style, her delightful characters sprang from her pen! "Their wild and crazy hair is a sign of strength," she thought, "and their crooked little smiles are endearing." She quickly identified the charming characters as Mother, Daughter, Sister, Father, Son, Friend, and so on until all the people and places in life were filled. Then, with her own loved ones in mind, she wrote a true and special sentiment to each one. This would be the beginning of a wonderful success story, which today still finds Marci writing each and every one of her verses in this same personal way.

Marci is a self-taught artist who has always enjoyed writing and art. She is thrilled to see how her delightful characters and universal messages of love have touched the hearts and lives of people everywhere. Her distinctive designs can also be found on Blue Mountain Arts greeting cards, calendars, bookmarks, and other gift items.

To learn more about Marci, look for Children of the Inner Light on Facebook or visit her website: www.MARCIonline.com.